THE CURSE
OF THE FROG PRINCE

W9-CCU-506

FROGGY RIBBIT'S TRUE TALES

Hello again! Our next True Tale comes from Fred Frog—the Frog Prince himself!

Fred, we know the stories. A princess kisses you and gets her prince. But now tell us what *really* happened.

Well, it was on my last birthday that my father told me . . .

So you finally got your princess. Are you happy with her?
Oh, she is nice. She feeds me. We go for long walks. She cleans up after me.

I just do not think she expected to end up with this kind of prince.
Come on, Prince—time to go walkies!
PRINCE

FALL FASHION

THE BEAR TRUTH

The following story is true. Only the words were changed to tell it.

ANOTHER CRIME SOLVED BY B.E.A.R.S.!